Farley
Follows His Nose

story by Lynn Johnston & Beth Cruikshank

illustrations by Lynn Johnston

The Bowen Press

An Imprint of HarperCollinsPublishers

Farley Follows His Nose

Copyright © 2009 by Entercom Canada, Inc.

Manufactured in China. All rights reserved.

No part of this book may be used or reproduced in any manner whatsoever without written permission except in the case of brief quotations embodied in critical articles and reviews. For information address HarperCollins Children's Books, a division of HarperCollins Publishers, 1350 Avenue of the Americas, New York, NY 10019.

www.harpercollinschildrens.com

Library of Congress Cataloging-in-Publication Data

Johnston, Lynn Franks, date

Farley follows his nose / by Lynn Johnston & Beth Cruikshank. — 1st ed.

p. cm.

Summary: Farley the dog follows his nose from one good smell to another all over town.

ISBN 978-0-06-170234-1 (trade bdg.)

[1. Dogs—Fiction.]   I. Cruikshank, Beth.   II. Title.

PZ7.J6448Far 2009   2008024713   [E]—dc22   CIP   AC

Typography by Rachel Zegar

1 2 3 4 5 6 7 8 9 10

❖

First Edition

To Lauren, Chris, and Arli,
and all the children who will read this book with them.

sniff snorfle **SNUFF**

It was a beautiful summer morning, and Farley's bath was over at last. Farley shook himself and drew in a deep breath. Baths always made Farley hungry, but in the breeze he smelled

rosesfreshcutgrasssweatypeoplethecatnextdoor

and . . .

...HOT DOGS!

Farley **LOVED** hot dogs.

Quickly, he followed his nose.

The scent got stronger as Farley ran.

Soon more delicious
smells mixed in:

sniff
snoof
snoof
Snuffa
WHUFF

hotdogsapplejuicelemoncakepopcorn

and . . .

...CHILDREN!

Farley
LOVED
children.

But the children were too busy to play with him.

lick
slorupp
slupp
SLURP

Except for one little boy,
who was sitting all alone.
Farley licked his face.

The boy gave Farley his hot dog. And
some popcorn. And a big piece of cake
with green and yellow icing.

Then the boy's mother saw Farley,
and she shouted in surprise.

Farley ran away as fast as he could.

When Farley stopped, he was in a new
part of town, and he was still hungry.

sniff
snerf
Snuffah
SNOOF

In the warm afternoon
air, he smelled

exhaustfumesgarbagehotrubbermarigolds

and . . .

...A HAM AND CHEESE SANDWICH!

Farley **LOVED** ham and cheese sandwiches.

"Where did you come from?" A trucker gave Farley some of his sandwich and said, "I could take you home, if you only had a name tag."

The ham and cheese sandwich was good, but it made Farley thirsty.

He walked on, getting thirstier and thirstier as the day grew hotter.

whuffa
snuffa
sniffah
snoofah
Snuff
SNIFF

Farley followed his nose. He smelled

freshpaintbananapeelspowertoolssawdust

and . . .

...A POOL!

Farley
LOVED
pools.

Now that he was no longer hungry or thirsty, Farley felt sleepy. He found a nice shady spot and dug a bed in the soft dirt.

In the cool evening air, he smelled pineneedleswetdirttomatoesmint and . . .

...TOASTED MARSHMALLOWS!

Farley
LOVED
marshmallows.

But "None for you," a girl said. "Dogs' stomachs aren't made for such sweet stuff."

Disappointed, Farley wandered away. At least the park was filled with interesting smells.

snuffah
whuffah
snoof
SNIFF

CHOCOLATE

Farley followed his nose. He found

awaterfountaincolacanscandywrappersrabbits

and . . .

...SOMEONE HIDING BEHIND A BUSH!

Farley
LOVED
playing hide-and-seek.

whiffa
sniffa
snerfah
snuffah
snifff
snuff
SNIFF

But the little boy was crying.
Farley didn't know what was wrong.
He checked the boy all over and smelled

Popcornlemoncakeapplejuicehotdogs

and . . .

. . . then Farley knew who it was! It was the little boy from the party!

"I'm lost, doggie!" the little boy cried. "It's dark and I'm scared and I want to go home."

snorfah
snoofa
whuffa
sniff
snuffle
whuffle
SNORT

All the good smells made Farley's mouth water. Maybe there were more hot dogs, lemon cake, and popcorn at the little boy's house!

Farley nudged the little boy up and sniffed the air. Farley followed his nose, and the little boy followed Farley.

Back they went, past the rabbit hole and the fountain and the marshmallow fire, past the shady spot and the pool and the sawdust smell.

They passed the marigolds and the hot rubber and the garbage.
Farley hesitated then, because that garbage smelled yummy.
But the little boy tugged on his fur, so he continued on.

The scent was there,
fainter now but still in the air:

popcornlemoncakeapplejuicehotdogs

They hurried forward.

When they reached the little boy's house, Farley stopped in surprise. The children were gone, and there were no hot dogs or lemon cake or popcorn.

But the little boy was happy. "You showed me the way home. I love you, doggie!" He hugged Farley and ran inside calling, "Mom! Dad! I'm home!"

Farley sighed. His friend had left, and he was hungry again. He was getting tired, too, and he missed his own family.

He walked sadly down the street, wondering where they were.

whuffa snuffa whuffa snuffa sniff snoof SNERF

In the dark night air, he smelled

hollyhockssquirrelsjuniperaftershave

and . . .

...PIZZA!

Farley
LOVED
pizza.

Most of all, he loved the pizza Uncle Phil sometimes
brought over. It smelled just like this.
Farley followed his nose.

And there was Uncle Phil! Farley was excited to see him. Uncle Phil was excited, too.

"Farley, you big mutt. Where have you been? We've been looking all over town for you!"

Uncle Phil didn't give Farley any pizza. But he put him in the car and took him home, which was even better.

Farley was so happy to be with his family again . . .

. . . and to see the supper waiting in his dish.

snniffffff?

Then Elly sniffed the air.

"Peeee-YEWWWW," Elly said.
"Farley, you need another bath!"